Joseph Fayrer

On the relation of filaria sanguinis hominis to the endemic diseases of India: read before the Epidemiological Society, February 5

Antigonos

Joseph Fayrer

On the relation of filaria sanguinis hominis to the endemic diseases of India: read before the Epidemiological Society, February 5

Reprint of the original, first published in 1879.

1st Edition 2024 | ISBN: 978-3-38801-009-0

Antigonos Verlag is an imprint of Outlook Verlagsgesellschaft mbH.

Verlag (Publisher): Outlook Verlag GmbH, Zeilweg 44, 60439 Frankfurt, Deutschland, info@outlook-verlag.de
Vertretungsberechtigt (Authorized to represent): E. Roepke, Zeilweg 44, 60439 Frankfurt, Deutschland
Druck (Print): Libri Plureos GmbH, Friedensallee 273, 22763 Hamburg, Deutschland

ON THE RELATION OF

FILARIA SANGUINIS HOMINIS

TO THE

ENDEMIC DISEASES OF INDIA.

*READ BEFORE THE EPIDEMIOLOGICAL SOCIETY,
FEBRUARY 5.*

BY

SIR JOSEPH FAYRER, K.C.S.I., M.D., F.R.S.

(*Reprinted from* THE MEDICAL TIMES AND GAZETTE)

LONDON
PARDON & SON, PRINTERS, PATERNOSTER ROW
—
1879

ON THE RELATION OF
FILARIA SANGUINIS HOMINIS TO THE
ENDEMIC DISEASES OF INDIA.

READ BEFORE THE EPIDEMIOLOGICAL SOCIETY, FEBRUARY 5.

By SIR JOSEPH FAYRER, K.C.S.I., M.D., F.R.S.

THE subject is so comprehensive that it would be impossible in the limits of an ordinary paper to do it justice; but as the Council of the Epidemiological Society has desired me to bring the matter before you, I proceed to draw attention to some aspects of an important helminthological discovery, and also to certain points in which, in its relation to endemic disease in India and other tropical and sub-tropical regions, further information may be anticipated.

I must say, at once, that I have nothing original of my own to communicate, but deal entirely with the work of others. I am glad to have this opportunity of testifying how deeply medical science is indebted to our brethren at home and abroad for their researches. I know of nothing that more practically illustrates the scientific zeal of our profession than the subject I have to bring before you.

In March, 1870, Dr. T. R. Lewis, of H.M.'s British Medical Service, made known his discovery of certain microscopic nematodes in chylous urine, and suggested their causal relation to that disorder system. In the Appendix to the Sixth Annual Report Sanitary Commissioner with the Government of India.

1869, published in Calcutta in 1870, he states that when examining the urine of a patient, in Calcutta, suffering from chyluria, he discovered, amidst the fibro-albuminous matter in that fluid, the embryos of a new round worm each time he repeated the examination, and noted appearances that indicated the existence of a sheath in which it was enclosed. He, at first, thought that what he saw were detached filaments of a fungus, but movements revealed their real nature.

As to their size, considering that 200 could pass abreast through a pin-hole, an orifice not exceeding one-fiftieth of an inch in diameter, it is not surprising that their existence had not been suspected. Lewis, I suppose, was not then aware that they had been seen, under similar circumstances, by Wucherer, in Bahia, in 1866. This appears to be the earliest notice of their existence in India, and certainly it was an original discovery of the greatest importance in its bearing on hitherto unsuspected causes of certain diseases. In July, 1872, when examining the blood of a native in the Calcutta Medical College Hospital, who was suffering from diarrhœa, Lewis detected nine nematoid worms in a state of great activity on a single slide. They were similar to those observed in chylous urine in March, 1870. Specimens were sent to Dr. Parkes, who, with Mr. Busk, expressed an opinion that they belonged to Filariæ. It had not hitherto been known that they were *hæmatozoa*. The name *Filaria sanguinis hominis* was given to them. Further examination of cases of chyluria proved that both in the blood and urine the filariæ were to be found, and also in morbid secretions. For example, in a case where chyluria was associated with granular eyelids and inflammation of the eyes, giving rise to a milky secretion from the corners of the eyelids, filariæ were detected in the exudation. Lewis gives a rough estimate of the number of filariæ at 140,000, being an allowance of two individuals in each drop of the ten pounds of blood possessed by a person of one hundred pounds weight. This—if the parasites pervade the whole blood, as they probably do,—is, I should think, considerably below the mark !

The creature is very minute, and apt to be overlooked without long, careful, and patient examination. The power employed should be sufficiently high to define a red blood-globule. The diameter of Filaria sanguinis hominis is about $\frac{1}{3500}$ inch—some are larger, some smaller: the largest $\frac{1}{3000}$ by $\frac{1}{68}$; the smallest $\frac{1}{7000}$ by $\frac{1}{123}$. Filaria sanguinis hominis belongs to a family that includes many other entozoa prejudicial to man, and animals—Ascaris, Oxyuris, Dochmius, Speiroptera, Anguillula (the diarrhœa worm of Cochin China), Dracunculus, Trichinæ. It is allied to the last-mentioned, and their larval forms are somewhat alike, though perfectly distinguishable. During the first few hours "after removal from the body, the filaria is in constant motion, coiling and uncoiling itself, and lashing the blood corpuscles about in all directions." It has the power of retracting the head and tail. When recent it is smooth and translucent; some have a granular appearance. A spot like an oral aperture sometimes appears. As they become inactive they lose their transparency; if a little spirit be added they preserve their outline, otherwise they quickly disappear. They are capable of retracting within the delicate sheath by which they are surrounded. Under careful examination an oral and an anal aperture and an intestinal tube can be made out.

The embryo being enclosed in a sheath, and having no visible boring apparatus, we may assume that its home is in the blood (or lymph), and that its movements are those of the circulation. With regard to the part taken by it in the production of disease, post-mortem evidence is much needed, not only with the view of determining what pathological changes take place, but of ascertaining the seat of the parent worm, and especially should search be made in and near the blood and lymph channels. Lewis describes the post-mortem appearances in the kidney. " It was more than usually lobulated, and on section several of the pyramids, especially near their apices, presented a smooth, tallowy appearance, suggestive of amyloid disease; no approach to the characteristic iodine reaction was obtained. Translucent oil-like tubules of a varicose appearance were observed alongside of the uriniferous tubes, as if the vessels had been plugged; boiling ether had no effect on them. No other morbid changes were found, but, in every part of the kidney examined, filariæ were found, as also in the branches of the renal artery, which were not, however, enlarged." The capillary vessels, from the absence of good preparation, were not examined. Such is the course of the hæmatozoon into the urine. Worms of various sizes were found in the chylous urine, but no casts.

Chyluria is frequently associated with symptoms of other obscure diseases—diarrhœa (often of a persistent character), deafness, chronic ophthalmia. And here I may notice that in horses (a), and men (b) too, in Africa and India, a filaria is occasionally found in the eyeball. I have several times seen horses blind from the presence of a living and moving nematode in the anterior chamber, which quickly induces corneal opacity. There are several other morbid conditions that I shall presently refer to.

The chyluria, due probably to the stoppage and rupture of lymphatic vessels, is doubtless very frequently associated with filaria; but we may not, I think, affirm that it is always so caused—other conditions may give rise to it; but in warm countries, or in cases of persons who have long resided in them, it is important to consider their possible origin, not only in chyluria, but in chronic diarrhœa, especially if associated with intermittent chyluria. It has been shown that the parasite may live for years without causing any very palpable derangement of health; and that it does not undergo any development as long as it remains in the circulation. It may continue an abiding source of disease, which, under certain conditions, will develope itself; and what these conditions are we now seek to learn. This is an important subject on which we seem likely to add to our knowledge.

There are others besides Lewis who share the honour of the discovery. The literature of the subject is already extensive. I can only refer to some of those who have contributed to it. Dr. Cobbold, who has himself added so largely to our knowledge, not only on this, but on all else connected with helminthology, gives a list of authors.

In 1843, Klenke found worms in the blood of a person suffering from vertigo, but as he did not describe them exactly, we cannot say if they were nematodes.

In 1866 or 1868, the late Dr. Wucherer, of Bahia, published an account of a worm that he had detected in the urine of a person suffering from hæmato-chyluria—he found it when searching for Bilharzia—and describes the minute nematodes as narrow at one, obtuse at the other extremity. He found them on subsequent examinations of chyluria, and they were always alive and active.

In 1868, Dr. Salisbury in the United States discovered a small entozoon in the bladder of a chylurious person. He described it as a new form, and called it Trichina cystica.

In July, 1870, Dr. Cobbold, F.R.S., found a minute nematode and eggs in the urine of a little girl from Natal suffering

---

(a) Filaria papillosa.(b) F. Loa.

from Bilharzia. He says that, though numbers of fluke's eggs were passed daily with much blood, it never occurred to him that the nematode was hæmatozoal. The child's parents had told him that she had passed three small worms by the urethra long before, and he assumed that they were of urinary origin. Had he, as he remarks, examined the blood from a finger, Lewis's important discovery of microscopic hæmatozoa might have been anticipated.

In or about 1872 several "finds" were made in foreign countries. I cannot detail them, but they will be found in Dr. Cobbold's interesting paper in the *Proceedings of the Linnæan Society* (October, 1878, vol. xiv., No. 76); and in a paper in the *Veterinarian*, a translation of a memoir by Da Silva Lima, with appendix by Le Roy de Méricour; also in the August and September numbers of *Archives de Médecine Navale*, by Bourel Ronciere.

Up to 1872 the discoveries had reference only to the urine. In July, 1872, however, Lewis discovered the nematode in the blood, under circumstances already described, in a case of diarrhœa, and in the following October in that of a formerly chylurious person. The worms were identical. This very important discovery of the *blood stage* is, therefore, Lewis's; although the embryo had been discovered some time previously in the urine by Wucherer.

The parent worm was discovered still later by Dr. Bancroft in Australia. Thus we have separate discoveries of the different phases of filaria from widely distant quarters of the globe.

Dr. Manson, in China, ascertained that the mosquito is its intermediary host. To all much credit is due; and whether we call the parasite *F. Wucherii, F. Sanguinis hominis* (Lewis), or *F. Bancroftii*, is unimportant. If the blood stage (which is by no means certain) be the most important phase of its genetic cycle, we may, perhaps with advantage, retain the Indian name; if the parent be the cause of most mischief, which may prove to be the case, then perhaps *Bancroftii* will be the most appropriate specific distinction. In any case, to each of these gentlemen is due the honour of a most important discovery.

To revert to the embryo, in 1874 Dr. Sonsino, in Egypt, when examining the blood of a young Egyptian Jew suffering from Bilharzia hæmaturia, detected a minute filarial embryo, which he was good enough to demonstrate to me in Cairo when I was there in 1876. I wrote a notice of it in the *Lancet* as Filaria sanguinis hominis Egyptiaca. It seemed probable that it was a variety; but there is, I believe, no doubt that it is identical with Lewis's species. Sonsino has also discovered a filaria embryo in the blood of the horse, and in the crow. He is adding, and will add, to our knowledge of the entozoa of that part of the world.

In 1875, Dr. O'Neill, in the South Coast of Africa, found embryo nematodes in the exudation from the skin in a disease named by the negroes *Craw-craw*; whilst Dr. Arango detected it at Bahia in a negro suffering from the same disease. He called it Filaria dermithemica. F. Dos-Santos found it, *once only*, in the blood of a person suffering from elephantiasis in Bahia. Dr. Crevaux detected it in chyluria in Guadaloupe.

Certain free microscopic nematodes very closely resembling, if not identical, have been found in the potable waters of Rio-Aqua di Carioca by Dr. Magalhaes. Their genetic relation with Filaria sanguinis hominis is not, I believe, quite established, but the indication is important, as it points to the channel through which the parasite may find entrance to the human body.

Dr. Manson, of Amoy, has discovered—what had been already suggested by Dr. Bancroft in Australia—that the hæmatozoa are passively transferred to the stomach of the mosquito, and he has described the transformation they there undergo. A new and important *rôle* for this already obnoxious insect has thus been revealed, the *full* import of which remains still to be ascertained. It appears that the mosquito has a peculiar facility for ingesting filariæ, as the blood taken from their stomachs contains more parasites than that in the person they have fed on. Manson says that the embryo, after entering the mosquito's stomach, retains for a short time the appearances which characterise it in the human blood. But after a few hours changes begin: a double outline of body, and marked striation, appear and again disappear. This is the first stage in metamorphosis, and occupies about thirty-six hours. It now enters on a sort of chrysalis condition, in which, though quiescent, it changes in form—its four-lipped mouth and an intestinal tract become apparent about the fourth or fifth day. The subsequent details are difficult to trace, but it is now one-fortieth to one-thirtieth of an inch in length; it now completes the mosquito-phase, and is very active, "moving about with great facility and rapidity in the water, into which it has emerged equipped for independent life."

Lewis also found the embryo in mosquitos in Calcutta, and has described them in the *Bengal Asiatic Society's Journal* of March, 1878. He says that most of them came from pariah dogs, and they very closely resembled the human parasite. But he says that the mosquitos captured in a particular servant's house did contain human filariæ, and that he had the opportunity of observing all the stages of their growth; that whilst the stomach digests some, others perforate the walls of the stomach, pass out, and undergo developmental changes in the thoracic and abdominal tissues of the insect. He thinks that it will be found that Manson's observations apply to India, but he does not feel convinced that the mosquito is *the* only intermediary host; it may turn out to be so, but it is to be noted that even the most advanced stage hitherto seen is still a very immature one, no trace of reproductive organs being distinguishable.

Dr. Cobbold thinks we have sufficient information to establish the genetic relationship between Filaria sanguinis hominis, the stomachal filaria of mosquito, and the sexually mature Filaria Bancroftii. This name is given by Dr. Cobbold to the mature worm in honour of its discoverer, who first found it in Australia in 1876. He sent specimens home, and they were verified by Drs. Cobbold and Roberts. Dr. Cobbold having detected, among specimens of microscopic hæmatozoa sent home by Bancroft, a single empty egg-covering, which corresponded with some he had observed in a Natal patient, suggested search for the parent; and Bancroft found it, in a person suffering from lymphatic abscess of the arm, in December, 1876. Lewis made further search, and on August 7, 1877, found two specimens in the blood-clot from a young Bengalli lad who had been operated on for nævoid elephantiasis. Carter, in India, in 1876, had also found it in a lymphatic abscess of the arm, and in hydrocele of spermatic cord. Drs. Arango and F. Dos-Santos and others also verified the discovery. Bancroft sent specimens to Dr. Cobbold, who gave an account of their anatomy in the *Lancet* of October, 1877, with figures. He only found the female, and gives the following dimensions:—Mature—length, $3\frac{1}{2}$ in.; breadth, 1″. Embryo—length, $\frac{1}{200}$th to $\frac{1}{125}$; breadth, $\frac{1}{3000}$ to $\frac{1}{2500}$. "Body capillary, smooth, uniform in thickness; head with a simple circular mouth, destitute of papillæ; neck narrow, about one-third of the width of the body. Tail of female simple, bluntly pointed. Reproductive outlet close to the head;

*

anus immediately above the tip of the tail. A number of ova and embryos escaped from a mature worm during examination."

Lewis also gave a description and figures in the *Lancet* of September 19, 1878, which very closely corresponds with that by Dr. Cobbold, and says, " It is possible that when the parasite discovered by Dr. Bancroft has been more definitely described, and its anatomy investigated, it may become evident that it is identical with the Filaria sanguinis hominis." Of this I imagine there is now little, if any, doubt. I should add that Lewis noticed that the embryos which escaped from the mature worm detected in the blood-clot of nævoid elephantiasis were identical with embryos found in the blood of other parts of the body.

As regards the mode of entry into the human body, Manson says, speaking of the embryo *after* it has left the mosquito and escaped into water, " It is through this medium brought into contact with the tissues of man, and thus, either by piercing the integuments, or, what is more probable, being swallowed, it works its way through the alimentary canal to its final resting-place; arrived there, its development is perfected, fecundation is effected, and finally the embryo filariæ we meet with in the blood are discharged in successful swarms, and in countless numbers. In this way the genetic cycle is completed." With regard to a boring apparatus Manson says, " I cannot say if the three or four papillæ round one extremity of the developed embryo constitute the perfected boring apparatus of the worm, or if it is a boring apparatus at all; but comparing this with what is found in other species, I think it very probable that it either is or will become the piercing apparatus."

I may not dwell longer on these details : they will be found in full in Dr. Manson's excellent paper in the *Linnæan Society's Journal*, No. 75, vol. xiv.

I would just remark that whilst this is probably the right interpretation of what takes place, it cannot yet be regarded as perfectly established until further observation shall have confirmed the facts.

This much, however, may be regarded as certain :—The embryo filariæ may swarm in the blood, and be associated with, or give rise to, certain morbid conditions. They pass into the mosquito, or it may be into other intermediary hosts, where they undergo developmental changes in the tissues of the insect, and are at length set free in the water along with the larvæ. We cannot actually trace them further, as they pass into man, but we have good grounds for believing that they do so through the medium of water. Nor can we follow them through the further developmental changes that result in sexual maturity ; though we know that the fully developed worm finds its home in the tissues of man, and then sheds its embryos into the circulating blood. How much, and in what proportion, the diseased conditions that result from their presence are due to the embryo, or how much to the parent worm, we are still unable to say; but we have good ground for believing that post-mortem examinations will now throw light on the subject, as well as on the precise localisation of the parent worm.

It is not within the scope of this paper to describe the diseases due to nematodes generally; I must restrict my remarks to those peculiar to Filaria sanguinis hominis (Lewis).

Great advances have been made in our knowledge of this subject during the last four or five years, in reference to the relation of this parasite to certain forms of tropical disease. It has been shown that disorders of the lymphatic system are most frequently associated with, if not caused by, Filaria : nævoid and ordinary elephantiasis Arabum (*perhaps* also elephantiasis Græcorum), (a) chyluria, hæmaturia, hydrocele and affections of the cord and testis, lymph-varix and abscess, diarrhœa, fever, cachexia, deterioration of general health, certain skin diseases (Craw-craw), deafness, eye disease—all these have been ascribed to it, though it is not asserted that they are *always* so caused. Being symptoms of impaired or impeded function, they may be produced otherwise; but it is tolerably certain that we have now got one explanation of their origin in a hitherto unsuspected agency. The mechanical action, were there no other effect, might explain much that occurs by the plugging and obstruction of the nutritive channels. To say nothing of the direct effects on the blood itself, one can hardly conceive that these organisms should exist in the blood in any numbers without affecting it prejudicially ; and yet we know that they have been found in the blood of persons who were apparently

---

(a) I find in the *Lancet* of February 1, 1879, that Dr. Bancroft has recently written to Dr. Cobbold that he had found filariæ in the blood taken from anæsthetic patches on the thigh of a European aged forty-nine, in Brisbane, suffering from leprosy. Dr. Bancroft also says that he has examined the blood of two patients who formerly had filariæ associated with abscess of the arm; their blood is now free from hæmatozoa.

healthy. Of course, it is difficult to define any absolute standard of perfect health; and there may be a considerable amount of cachexia, even in persons generally regarded as healthy—though, perhaps, could we know their real condition, we might think otherwise. What the peculiar change in locality or action on the part of the hæmatozoon may be that determines the diseased condition, we are still ignorant; and this is just one of the points that needs elucidation.

We naturally ask if there be any analogy in the conduct of other entozoa in this respect; and in comparative helminthology also we look for guidance. Dracunculus may cause little or no annoyance in the earlier stages; but developing, changing place, and discharging its embryos, the gravest results accrue. So Trichina, which in its earlier stages is comparatively unfelt, may become the cause of fatal disease.

When the blood swarms with minute organisms, one might expect to find some evidence of their presence, either from mechanical interference with the blood or lymph circulation, or from *direct action on the blood itself*, or on the nerve-centres. Of the first we have an example in lymph-scrotum, elephantiasis, and chyluria. Of the second, I believe it is probable that several morbid states hitherto ascribed to other causes are due; and, judging from analogy, we may believe this is so. We know how severely animals suffer from the presence in the blood of other minute organisms. Anthrax, for example, is produced by Bacillus; a cholera-like disease in pigs is produced by the migration of Stephanurus, as pointed out by Dr. Cobbold; phthisis in sheep by Strongylus filaria; and in man, as shown by Griesinger, the so-called and widely spread Egyptian chlorosis owes its origin to Dochmius duodenalis (Leukhart), and that not only anæmia, but liver disease and a form of dysentery, are produced by the same parasite, which is not very unlike Filaria sanguinis hominis. "Similar facts," says De Chaumont, "have been observed in Brazil, Arabia, Madagascar: it seems impossible but that in India the formidable affections caused by the Dochmius should be common."

Manson and Lewis have shown that certain filariæ (*F. sanguinolenta* and *F. immitis*) infest dogs in China and India; they very closely resemble the human parasite, and give rise to certain diseases. Sonsino has demonstrated filariæ in the horse and crow in Egypt. In July, 1872, Lewis found in the exudation pressed out from the mesenteric glands of a pariah dog, in Bengal, a small embryo nematode that very closely resembled the Filaria sanguinis hominis, and corresponding to Filaria sanguinolenta of Rudolphi. They were found also in connexion with the walls of the stomach and œsophagus, as had been stated by Czernay and others; in the walls of the bloodvessels, especially of the thoracic aorta; in the interior of fibrous tumours of from the size of a pea to that of a filbert, or even of a walnut. On the walls and in the substance of the coats of the vessel there might be seen a pitted or sacculated or atheromatous condition of the inner coat. There was also an enlargement and softening of glandular structures near the base of the heart.

The tumours of the aorta afforded opportunity of studying the growth of the parasite from an early period up to maturity, as specimens of almost every stage of development may be found lodged in the walls of a single aorta. The parasite is found coiled up in the tumour. They are immature, $\frac{1}{10}$th of an inch in length, $\frac{1}{150}$th in breadth; some smaller. When at this stage they moult; further changes take place, and by the time the worm has become three-quarters of an inch long, reproductive organs can be made out. It now gradually acquires a pinkish colour, and instead of occupying a small tumour alone, it joins other worms in a larger tumour, each occupying a different tunnel. Sometimes they make their way outside. When mature the worm is from three-quarters of an inch to one inch long, and one-fortieth of an inch broad. The female is two to three inches in length. They were also found in the thoracic glands and stomach. The *ova* are oval, $\frac{1}{200}$ of an inch in size. When crushed, an *inactive* embryo escaped. Lewis has doubts as to the habitat of these embryos, whether the moist earth, the water, or the intestinal tube of some other creature; but we have thus the opportunity of watching the development of the *sexually mature* worm. Manson made similar investigations on Chinese dogs, and found Filaria sanguinolenta associated with Filaria immitis. The free embryos in the blood of such dogs are probably the progeny of either or both—Filaria immitis and Filaria sanguinolenta. It is said that Filaria sanguinolenta is oviparous, whilst Filaria immitis is viviparous. Filaria immitis is larger than Filaria sanguinolenta. It is found in the mature form *in the heart* of the dog, and its broods of embryos swarm in their blood. Time does not permit of my dwelling on these canine filariæ. I have only done so, so far, in regard to their analogy with the human parasite, which probably, in its mature form, leads a similar existence, shedding its broods of embryos into the bloodvessels or lymphatics.

Dr. Manson describes the following diseased conditions in dogs caused by filariæ :—Filaria sanguinolenta gives rise to three serious morbid states—(1) stricture of œsophagus; (2) pleurisy; (3) paralysis of hind legs—caused by the presence of the worm in the tissues about the œsophagus, forming tumours—tumours bursting into the pleura—plugging of the capillaries of spinal cord by ova, etc.; and other affections that may be produced by them in the intestines, kidneys, or other viscera. The Filaria immitis, on the other hand, affects the heart and lungs. By arrest in the lungs they give rise to tuberculoid tissue, at all events an infiltration resembling miliary tuberculosis; but more frequently they manifest themselves in the heart's action by interfering with the integrity of the valves, or the capacity of the pulmonary artery or its branches. Death not unfrequently results suddenly; or there is a gradual failing of circulation and respiration, ending in death. Such animals are short-winded, and liable to attacks of syncope. And one can readily imagine many other complications arising in one so affected; and it is said that two-thirds of them are so in China, where they frequently are the subject of *both* filariæ.

Their mere *presence*, even in great numbers, does not necessarily produce symptoms of disease; and this is very remarkable when we consider the demand these creatures may make and the changes they may effect in the nutritive fluids. It is interesting to notice the action of other allied forms in man—*e.g.*, Trichinæ and Dracunculus behave nearly in the fashion of Filaria sanguinolenta in the dog: they migrate, pierce the tissues, develope, burst, and give exit to embryos, which set up irritation, perhaps induce pain and other secondary affections, to say nothing of those caused by their immediate presence; and yet there is a period in their existence, too, during which there is little, if anything, to indicate their presence. Recently we have learned from the French physicians Drs. Normond and Bavay of new minute nematodes from Cochin China—the Anguillula stercoralis, and A. intestinalis. The former, found in the stomach, the whole length of the intestine, pancreatic and gall ducts, is 1 millimetre in length, and 0·04 broad; the latter, in the hepatic duct, walls of gall-bladder, but less frequently than the former, is three times its length, and sixty-five times its breadth. These are described as giving rise to dysenteric diarrhœa, which is very intractable and apt to end in marasmus. You will find a description of this parasite in the *Archives de Médecine Navale* for September, 1878.

But we have still much to learn about these human nematodes, especially in regard to their mode of entry into the body, their locality, habitat, and the way in which they become sexually mature, where and when fecundated, and when precisely the embryos are let loose among the tissues, and how they find their way into the blood- and lymph-vessels, and the precise relation that these vessels bear to each other as carriers of the ova in the embryos. The subject is in the hands of competent observers, and we may look with confidence for a solution of most of what now seems obscure, especially from India, where post-mortem examinations apparently are more easily obtained than in China.

I have given a brief outline of the principal facts relating to the human-blood filaria ; and have alluded to some connected with its congeners that affect the lower animals, so far, at least, as they throw light on what is obscure in the human parasite. It remains to be shown what we already know, and in what direction we are to look for further information. I have said that Filaria is frequently associated with, if not the actual cause of, chyluria and other disturbances of the lymphatic system; it is on this part of the economy, indeed, that its influence is specially exerted. Some years ago, in writing about Nævoid Elephantiasis, I said that I thought it probable that other forms of disease would prove to be due to Filaria, and recent observations confirm the prediction. I repeated the observation in 1876, when writing on Sonsino's discovery of the Filaria in Egypt; and, almost daily, proof is forthcoming that in it is to be found the explanation of much that has hitherto been etiologically uncertain. I believe that we are still only on the threshold of our discoveries in regard to this form of helminthiasis. When we consider how much has already been traced to this parasite, it is impossible not to infer that more will be revealed.

Dr. Bancroft suggests that the following conditions are probably associated with Filaria:—Chyluria, hæmaturia, anæmia, tuberculosis, hydrocele with milky fluid, varicocele, elastic tumours in axilla and groin (Helminthiasis elastica), lymph-vesicles bursting in scrotum and abdomen, skin disease (Crawcraw), acute orchitis, lymphangitis with fever, erysipelatous lymphangitis leading to hypertrophy of skin (elephantoid fever, in short), elephantiasis of scrotum and leg, contraction of lymphatic trunks with neuralgic pains, abscess of scrotum, of glands of neck (like struma), of the lymphatics of the arm and thigh, intra-pelvic abscess, peculiar steatoma of face, venous varix, cerebral abscess, and other lesions of brain—a long list, suggestive of mechanical interference with the free passage of the nutritive fluids.

Manson's experience in China, and that of Lewis, McLeod, McConnell, Ewart, Carter, Palmer, and others, in India, shows that elephantiasis, nævoid and simple, is associated with filaria, and probably to these may be added other affections of the lymph system. My impression is that other morbid conditions—tropical cachexiæ, nervous disorders, paraplegia, and others; inflammation of serous and gastro-intestinal mucous membranes; diarrhœa, and certain forms of dysentery—may be due to it, directly or indirectly. Beri-beri, anasarca, dropsy, albuminuria, hæmaturia, may, like chyluria, receive a new explanation. The vague chronic ailments that sometimes adhere to old residents in tropical or sub-tropical climates may, in some instances, depend on the past or actual presence of these hæmatozoa. There are certain forms of hydrocele, epididymitis, and inflammatory conditions of the spermatic cord and its appendages, peculiar to tropical climates, that long puzzled me as to their etiology, which now begin to appear more easily accounted for—the tendency of the blood to form fibrinous coagula while within the walls of the living vessels and heart; the embolism, thrombosis, cardiac and pulmonary arterial pluggings; the arterial, venous, and capillary obstructions resulting in death; apnœa, gangrene, softenings, ulceration. That peculiar tendency in the blood of persons in malarious climates, notably Bengal, to form these fibrinous clots in the heart and pulmonary artery, so often fatal,—may it too, in some measure, be referred to the same cause, not always surely, but probably in some cases? I merely suggest it as worthy of consideration. The dogs in China die suddenly from the occurrence of interference with the heart's action due to filaria—whether to the direct mechanical interference, or to altered conditions of the blood, I cannot say; but what occurs in the dog may, from a similar cause, occur in man. At all events, I know from experience that men do so die and suffer in Bengal. Whether they are filarious or not remains to be shown. Had I known of its existence when I had such cases I should certainly have looked for it; and may it not be possible that such conditions as result from obstructed capillaries—boils, anthrax, local death of tissue, abscesses, ulcers (whether of skin or other tissue, the viscera themselves)—are so caused? The bloodvessels, too, may suffer from aneurism, varix, or some other condition of disease. In the dog they are so affected. So with stricture of the œsophagus, may we not, I repeat, in the present imperfect state of our knowledge, look for similar diseased conditions in man? Analogy warrants it, I think. Manson says that in the blood of 670 persons examinéd, of whom 195 were in apparently good health, he discovered filariæ fifty-three times associated with some morbid state, and nine times coexistent with the appearance of perfect health. Here is the list of what he found :—

	No. of cases.
Elephantiasis of scrotum	3
,, of leg	1
Lymph-scrotum and chyluria	2
,, ,, elephantiasis	1
,, ,, inguinal varix	1
Lymphatic inguinal varix	7
,, ,, ,, { coexistent with ulcer of cornea }	2
Hæmatemesis	1
Cataract	1
Ulcer of leg	4
Hydrocele	3
,, and rheumatism	1
,, and cataract	1
Rheumatism	1
Tumefaction of spleen	1
Fever and anasarca	1
Leprosy	2
Debility	1
Intermittent fever	2
,, ,, with enlarged spleen	1
,, ,, with inflamed scrotum	1
Hydrocele and fever	1
Chronic eczema	1
Internal hæmorrhoids	1
Stricture of œsophagus	1
Heart disease and ulcer	1
Total	53
Free from apparent disease	9
	62

It would seem that many forms of disease may be associated with, if not caused by, the parasite in one or other of its genetic phases. It is necessary to be careful lest, in the enthusiasm of a new discovery, too universal application be made of it, and more ascribed to it than is its due.

Important questions arise out of the preceding considerations. 1. Whence does Filaria come? 2. What can we do to prevent or remove it?

The second question will be best answered when we are able to reply satisfactorily to the first. When we know the origin and are assured of all the genetic phases, the whole life-history, we shall be in a better position to deal with it. Prevention is the first desideratum, but when infection has occurred we need some effective parasiticide; and it is not improbable that such exists. Perhaps carbolic or sulphurous acid, arsenic, or it may be some of the remedies that have proved useful as antiperiodics or febrifuges, may have owed some of their virtues to their anti-hæmatozoal properties. Secondary consequences, such as described in Manson's list, may be treated on ordinary medical and surgical principles, which at present I cannot stop to describe.

The area of distribution of these diseases is said to correspond with the geographical distribution of Culex. Where the mosquito is rare the diseases of Filaria are infrequent, and conversely. Manson advocates this view, and is impressed with the importance of the part played by the mosquito as intermediary host and propagator of the parasite. He certainly has grounds both in fact and analogy for his belief. Dracunculus employs the microscopic crustacean Cyclops as an intermediary host. Its second stage is thus, like that of Filaria, passed in another creature. They both find their way, through the medium of water, back to man. He adduces an authenticated instance of importation of the disease of elephantiasis by a single individual into Barbadoes. The mosquitos sucked his blood, and with it embryo filariæ; they were thus disseminated, and the disease has been ever since endemic in the island, where it was before unknown. I cannot affirm that the dissemination actually took place through the mosquito, but the rest of the story is authentic —the appearance in the island of elephantiasis with the advent of a particular individual. Dr. Manson thought the mosquito did it: if that be not the real explanation, I know no other. In any case, whatever part the mosquito may play, the water must be regarded with grave suspicion, and the greatest care observed in securing its purity; whilst, in view of what we know of the mosquito, it is desirable that he should be kept from access to all water supplies for either drinking or bathing, and that the water should be boiled before using. Sanitary science has already reduced the death-rate of our soldiers in India from 60 to 16 per 1000. May it here achieve further triumphs! It will do well, at all events, not only to insist on pure water, as it always does, but to keep its eye on mosquitos, and other possible intermediary pests. The usual way of getting rid of an entozoal pest is to interfere with its genetic cycle.

In concluding my remarks, I would say that I feel it is presumptuous to suggest any line of investigation; the discoveries of the Filaria and its relation to disease are so complete as far as they have gone, that it seems hardly right to trespass on ground so originally and advantageously occupied. I know that I have most imperfectly represented the work already done, and the only justification I have for dealing with the subject at all is obedience to your behests, and that, having had considerable experience of the diseases ascribed to Filaria, I am so far qualified to express my sense of the value of the light that has been thrown on a very obscure subject. I therefore esteem it no less a privilege than a duty to declare how much pathology is indebted to the knowledge gained. I am aware that the subject is still in its infancy, and that further research may modify much we now seem to know; but we are on a new and original track, and if I mistake not, one that will lead to important results— new explanations of the cause of disease, new methods of prevention and treatment, it may be—that will be as beneficial to mankind as they are honourable to those who pointed out the way to obtain them.

In congratulating ourselves that our own countrymen have taken so distinguished a part in these researches, and whilst giving all honour to our French, American, and Brazilian *confrères*, we cannot but feel satisfaction in remembering how much our distinguished countryman at home has done for the elucidation of this and all other forms of helminthiasis. His researches are, happily, well known throughout the scientific world. I wish I could add that they are as universally appreciated as they deserve. It has been the lot of other investigators that recognition of their labours has been long postponed, as it has been in Dr. Cobbold's case, but the time will certainly come, perhaps is now at hand, when they will be appreciated at their real value. Meanwhile he may feel the satisfaction of knowing that he has done great service to medicine; and I am glad of this opportunity of expressing not only my own personal obligation to him for valuable information often most kindly and freely given, but my admiration—which I know is shared by others—for the valuable information on this subject that he and others, notably Lewis, Wucherer, Bancroft, and Manson, have placed within our reach.

LONDON : PARDON AND SON, PRINTERS, PATERNOSTER ROW.